Depression

What It Is, How to Beat It

Linda Wasmer Smith

Enslow Publishers, Inc.

40 Industrial Road   PO Box 38
Box 398   Aldershot
Berkeley Heights, NJ 07922   Hants GU12 6BP
USA   UK

http://www.enslow.com

For Amanda and Michael, Ashley, and Ryan

Library of Congress Cataloging-in-Publication Data

Smith, Linda Wasmer.
    Depression : what it is, how to beat it / Linda Wasmer Smith
       p. cm. — (Teen issues)
    Includes bibliographical references and index.
    Summary: Describes the difference between simply feeling blue and having
clinical depression, details the different types of clinical depression along with their
symptoms and treatments, and provides information on getting help and relieving
stress.
    ISBN 0-7660-1357-X
    1. Depression, Mental Juvenile Literature. 2. Depression, Mental—Treatment
Juvenile Literature. [Depression, Mental.] I. Title. II. Series.
RC537.S587   2000
616.85'27—dc21   99-16473
                                    CIP

Printed in the United States of America

10 9 8 7 6 5 4 3 2 1

To Our Readers:
All Internet addresses in this book were active and appropriate when we went to press.
Any comments or suggestions can be sent by e-mail to Comments@enslow.com or to the
address on the back cover.

Illustration Credits: © Corel Corporation, p. 9; Skjold Photos, pp. 19, 25, 32, 42.

Cover Illustration: Portrait by Ed French; Background © Corel Corporation.

Contents

1

Blues, Blahs, or Depression?

Everyone gets the blues now and then. A person might feel sad or cranky, or he or she might feel as if nothing really matters. It is perfectly normal to be sad and down at times. However, when the low mood lasts for more than a couple of weeks, the problem may be depression. It is one of the most painful—but also most common and treatable—of all mental health problems.[1]

Depression is a medical illness, not a sign of personal weakness. It can be treated, so most people start feeling better in just a few weeks. Depression can strike anyone of any age, race, or sex. It can affect a person's feelings, thoughts, and behavior, and it may contribute to problems with relationships, grades, alcohol, drugs, or sex. Likewise, depression may lead to suicide,[2] the third leading cause of death for people ages fifteen to twenty-four.[3]

Justin's Story

Each person is different, and so is each episode of depression. Justin's case is fairly typical, however. He first began struggling with depression at age fourteen, when he was a freshman in high school. He felt sad most of the time, often for no obvious reason. He was restless and cranky, and he had trouble sleeping. Unfortunately, Justin did not get help right away. Without treatment, his problems just grew worse with time. By age sixteen, he says, "things had gotten really bad. Thoughts of death took up much of my day." By senior year, "I found it hard to think about anything other than my problems. I dropped from seventh place in my class to fortieth."

Justin's depression, left untreated, affected his relationships with those closest to him. "People sometimes told me that I scared them," he says. "I had dark moods, and I think that made people shy away from me. Also, my ex-girlfriend found me to be very emotionally draining at times. She didn't know how to deal with my problems, and I think that had a lot to do with our breakup after four years." Today, at age eighteen, four years after the depression started, Justin is finally planning to seek treatment and is hoping to get his life back on track.[4]

What Is Depression?

Justin had many of the classic symptoms of depression. When doctors talk about depression, they mean that a person either feels low or loses interest in nearly all activities, and this mood lasts for at least two weeks. The person in a low mood may feel sad or cry a lot. Sometimes a teenager or child may show sadness by becoming easily angered or annoyed. A depressed person also has several other symptoms, such as feelings of worthlessness, thoughts of death, or changes in eating, sleeping, thinking, movement, or energy level. This is known more formally as major depression.[5] It is also sometimes called clinical depression, which just means depression that is severe enough to need treatment.[6]

Some people have just one bout of depression, but for many others the problem comes and goes. Repeat attacks may occur close together, or they may be separated by many years. A single attack usually lasts six months or longer if not treated, but treatment can shorten the course of the illness.[7] A young person who has experienced major depression is at high risk of becoming depressed again within five years.[8]

What Are SAD and Dysthymia?

In certain people, major depression follows a seasonal pattern, usually coming in the fall or winter and leaving in the spring. Common symptoms include lack of energy, sleeping too much, overeating, weight gain, and a craving for sugary and starchy foods.[9] This kind of depression is known as seasonal affective disorder (appropriately abbreviated SAD). It seems to be linked to the decreased amount of sunlight that is available as the days grow shorter in winter.[10] An estimated 10 million Americans suffer from SAD. This includes about 3 percent of children and teenagers ages nine to seventeen.[11]

Depression can take other forms as well. Sometimes a person has a low mood that is milder and involves fewer symptoms than major depression but lasts for at least a year or two. This is known as dysthymia. It can be thought of as a slight case of depression that continues for a very long time. About 3 percent of Americans suffer from dysthymia, which often begins early in life. These are people who seem just a little down in the dumps but never seem to cheer up for long, even after months or years have passed.

Teenagers and children who have dysthymia are usually cranky as well as blue. They often have low self-esteem and a dark outlook on life. They may think that nothing they do is ever good enough, and they may spend a lot of time brooding about mistakes made in the past.

A person with dysthymia always has at least two of these symptoms: decreased appetite or overeating, trouble falling or staying asleep or sleeping too much, tiredness or loss of energy, low self-esteem, trouble concentrating or making decisions, and feelings of hopelessness. These symptoms last for at least a year in teenagers and children or two years in adults. During this period, the symptoms never disappear for more than two months at a time. They cause the person serious distress, or they interfere with personal relationships, school, or work.[12]

What Is Bipolar Disorder?

In some people, the terrible lows of major depression take turns with awful highs, known as mania. The person's mood swings from down to up and back again, with normal periods in between. The mood extremes may be mild or severe, and the mood changes may occur slowly or quickly. This roller-coaster illness is known as manic depression or, more formally, bipolar disorder. At least 2 million Americans suffer from bipolar disorder. For reasons that are still unclear, it usually begins during the teen years or early adulthood.[13]

In medical terms, mania refers to an overly high or irritable mood that lasts for at least one week or leads to

Seasonal affective disorder, a form of depression, is linked to the decreased amount of sunlight available as the days grow shorter in winter.

dangerous behavior. The person in a manic mood also has several other symptoms, such as inflated self-esteem, risk-taking behavior, or changes in sleeping, talking, thinking, or activity level.[14]

Teenagers in the grip of mania may seem unusually happy, silly, or very irritable. They may have an unrealistically high opinion of themselves, such as thinking that they have a special link to God. They may also have a great burst of energy, going with little or no sleep for days without feeling tired. These teenagers may talk too much or too fast or change topics too quickly. Their attention may jump constantly from one thing to another. They may take wild risks, such as driving recklessly, spending freely, having sex, or even jumping off a roof in the belief that they will not be hurt.[15] Of course, many teenagers act a little reckless on occasion; it is only when a number of symptoms are combined, and when they last for several days or become dangerous, that the problem is considered mania.[16]

How Are the Types Related?

Major depression, SAD, dysthymia, and the depressed periods in bipolar disorder are all closely related. SAD is major depression that comes and goes with the seasons. The depressed periods in bipolar disorder are bouts of major depression that take turns with bouts of mania. Dysthymia has symptoms much like those of major depression, but they are milder and fewer and continue for a long time. In this book, the word *depression* is used as a blanket term for all of these conditions. Because these types of depression are so closely linked, most information about symptoms, diagnosis, and treatment applies to all of them. When information does apply just to SAD, dysthymia, or bipolar disorder, it is noted.

What Is Not Depression?

True depression is different from ordinary moodiness. When doctors talk about a mood, they mean a long-lasting emotion that colors the way a person sees the world. Some people think that staying in a black mood for a long time is normal for teenagers, but this is not true. It may be a sign of a mood disorder—a mental illness in which the main feature is an abnormal mood—such as depression or mania.[17]

Of course, everyone feels down in the dumps at times. Normal sadness does not last long, though, and it does not go along with the other symptoms of depression. It also does not cause serious distress or interfere with personal relationships, school, or work. These are signs that depression may be a real concern.

Depression is also different from ordinary grief. It is perfectly natural to mourn when a loved one dies. A person may even have some of the symptoms of depression. This is quite normal. It may be time to seek help, however, if the symptoms last for longer then two months after the loss. Other signs of possible trouble include frequent feelings of worthlessness, thoughts of suicide, slowed down speech or movements, or problems at home, school, or work.[18]

What Causes Depression?

Depression is not a sign of personal failure. It is a myth that people who are depressed can just snap out of it if only they would try. Instead, depression is an illness, just as the measles and the flu are illnesses. Depression has been linked to an imbalance in neurotransmitters, the natural chemicals that let brain cells talk with one another. Scientists are also looking for a possible link between depression and other body chemicals called hormones.[19]

Yet, depression is not caused by any one factor. Other factors—such as family history, personality, and stress—may also play a role. Depression seems to run in some families. That is, people with relatives who have suffered from depression are more likely to become depressed themselves. However, many people with a family history of depression never get the illness.

People who have low self-esteem and a dark outlook on life are also more likely to become depressed. In addition, the illness may be linked to the way people handle stress. Depression is often triggered by a stressful event, such as the death of a loved one or a failure in school. However, depression can also occur for no obvious reason when life seems to be smooth sailing.[20]

Research on Gender Differences

Before age eleven, girls and boys have about equal rates of depression. By age eighteen, girls are twice as likely as boys to have the illness. Susan Nolen-Hoeksema, a psychologist at the University of Michigan, is studying possible reasons for

Who Gets Depressed?

Depression may affect as many as one in eight teenagers.[21] In all, it affects more than 17 million Americans each year.[22]

Depression is about twice as common in women as it is in men. This gender difference begins during the teen years. There are probably many reasons for the difference. For one thing, girls and boys may face different stresses. Both sexes must cope with issues such as finding an identity, dealing with sexuality, separating from parents, and making big decisions for the first time. However, society may have different expectations about these issues for girls and for boys.

Biological differences between the sexes may also play a role in depression. Some scientists are now looking for a possible link between depression and female hormones. A woman's hormones are affected by such things as pregnancy, childbirth, and the menstrual cycle.[23] It is already known that a small number of women become depressed within four weeks after giving birth. This is called postpartum depression. In addition, some women seem to have severe, regular mood changes just before their menstrual periods that can include depressed feelings.[24]

this change. She thinks that one reason for this increase may be gender differences in worrying. In Nolen-Hoeksema's research, girls reported they worried more than boys about their looks, friends, romance, personal problems, family problems, being liked, being safe, and what kind of person they are.[25]

What Is the Bottom Line?

About 25 percent of all women and 12 percent of all men will suffer from depression at some point in their life.[26] This illness can strike anyone of any age, race, or economic group. The good news is that millions of people have fought the battle against depression and many have won. Help is out there for those who ask.[27]

2

Yellow Lights, Red Flags

The blues and the blahs are feelings that happen inside a person, but they often lead to behaviors that can be seen on the outside. Different people show depression in different ways. Here are some ways in which the symptoms of depression may show up in a person's actions or words.

Depressed Mood

People who are depressed may say that they feel sad or empty, or they may cry a lot. These people may also describe themselves as hopeless, discouraged, or down in the dumps. However, not everyone behaves this way. Many teenagers show that they are depressed by being cranky, getting angry quickly, or staying angry a long time. They may act annoyed over little things that once would not have bothered them. Some depressed teenagers complain about unexplained aches and pains, such as headaches or stomach pains.[1] Others go out of their way to pick fights at home, even though they may be able to control their temper in public places, such as at school.[2]

Research on Physical Symptoms

Teenagers who are depressed may have vague aches and pains for which the doctor cannot find a physical cause. Psychiatrist Gail Bernstein of the University of Minnesota has studied the link between depression, anxiety, and physical symptoms among teenagers who missed lots of school. She found that the more severe the depression and anxiety, the worse the symptoms, which included dizziness, upset stomach, back pain, stomachache, vomiting, and menstrual problems.[3]

Loss of Interest

Some depressed people stop taking part in activities they once enjoyed, including music, sports, school clubs, or social activities. Teenagers who used to hang out with friends much of the time may start spending most of their time alone. They may give various excuses for withdrawing, such as lack of time or not feeling well. They may also describe themselves as having no feelings anymore. To some depressed people life seems meaningless, as if nothing good is ever going to happen again. Such people may describe life as pointless, hopeless, or unfair.[4] They may say that no one loves them or gripe that everything is boring or dumb.[5]

Changes in Eating

Many depressed people lose their appetite and eat much less than usual. They may say they feel as if they have to force themselves to eat. Others, however, eat much more. They may crave particular foods, such as sweets. Over time, changes in eating can lead to weight gain, or weight loss without dieting. Young people who are still growing may fail to gain weight as quickly as expected.[6] A craving for sugary or starchy foods is especially common in seasonal affective disorder (SAD).[7]

Changes in Sleeping

Many depressed people wake up in the middle of the night or too early in the morning, then cannot get back to sleep. Others lie awake for hours, unable to fall asleep in the first place. Still others sleep too much. Oversleeping is especially common in people suffering from SAD.[8] No matter how early they go to bed, they have trouble getting up the next morning. In some teenagers, the sleep cycle becomes so mixed up that they sleep during the day and stay awake all night. Depressed people often complain that they have nightmares. Even after a full night's sleep, they may find that they still are not rested the next day.[9]

Changes in Movement

Depression can affect the speed at which a person thinks, moves, or speaks. Some depressed people seem restless or unable to sit still. They may pace, fidget, wring their hands, or fiddle with their clothes, hair, or other objects. Others seem slowed down, as if they were moving in slow motion. They may speak slowly and softly, with long pauses before answering a question or responding to a request. They may also talk less than usual or about fewer things.[10] In addition, they may take an unusually long time to do simple things, such as getting dressed.[11]

Changes in Energy

Depressed people often complain about having low energy or feeling tired all the time. Even the smallest tasks seem to be a huge effort. Such people may be worn out by something as minor as taking a bath.[12] As a result, they may become couch potatoes who do little more than lie around and watch television or listen to music. Some depressed people have daily cycles in energy level. They may notice that they have more pep either in the morning or in the afternoon. While many people who are not depressed also notice such cycles, these changes in energy are combined with other symptoms in people who are depressed.[13]

Feelings of Worthlessness

Depressed people often describe themselves as being no good. They may say they have lost their confidence or blame themselves for things beyond their control, such as their parents' divorce.[14] Since they think they will not be as good as everyone else, they may be slow to join in activities. When they do take part, they may be overly critical of their own performance. If they fail at a task, they may say it is proof of their worthlessness. Such people may be supersensitive to even mild criticism. They may brood for a long time over tiny slights. They may also feel very guilty about small failings and seek harsh punishment.[15]

Changes in Thinking

Depressed people may have trouble thinking clearly, paying attention, or remembering things. This can lead to a sudden drop in grades at school.[16] Teenagers who have trouble making decisions may turn to parents or other adults for help.[17] Some people are unable to concentrate because their mind is filled with thoughts of sadness, worthlessness, or guilt. Such people find it hard to do even simple things.[18]

Thoughts of Death

Depressed people often think a lot about death and dying. Teenagers may spend lots of time listening to music or reading books that deal with such themes. They may frequently talk about what happens to people when they die or their fear that loved ones might be killed.[19] Depressed people may also have thoughts of suicide or make actual suicide plans. They may say other people would be better off if they were dead. In the worst case, they may act upon plans to kill themselves. Suicidal thoughts, words, or actions should always be taken seriously.[20]

Warning Signs of Depression

When a person is depressed, he or she may exhibit the following symptoms: feeling sad or crying a lot and finding that the problem does not go away; getting irritated or often losing his or her temper over little things; not wanting to do many of the things he or she used to like; feeling as if he or she wants to be left alone most of the time; thinking that life is meaningless, hopeless, or unfair; finding himself or herself eating or sleeping too little or too much; feeling restless or tired for no reason most of the time; feeling guilty without reason or as if he or she is worthless; having trouble paying attention or making up his or her mind; and thinking about death often or having thoughts of suicide.[21]

A person who is depressed may feel sad and hopeless and may withdraw from friends and family.

What About Suicide?

Suicide is most often caused by untreated depression.[22] It is the second leading cause of death among college students, the third leading cause of death for people ages fifteen to twenty-four, and the fourth leading cause of death for people ages ten to fourteen.

Suicide is the most serious consequence of depression. In recent years, the rate of suicide has been rising at a frightening pace among young people. The suicide rate for white males ages fifteen to twenty-four has tripled since 1950. For white females in this age group, it has more than doubled. For African-American males in this age group, it has risen by two thirds in only the past fifteen years. Boys are five times more likely to die from suicide than girls,[23] but girls attempt it twice as often.[24]

As many as one third of young people who commit suicide have made a previous attempt. Most suicide victims suffer from depression, substance abuse problems, or behavior problems at the time of their death. Often, the person has just gotten into some kind of trouble or has had a recent setback or rejection.[25]

Warning Signs of Suicide

Warning signs that a person may be suicidal include the following: being depressed; abusing alcohol or drugs; acting out of control; suffering a recent humiliation or loss, such as a romantic breakup;[26] making suicide threats or comments such as "I might as well be dead"; trying suicide in the past, even if the attempt did not seem very serious; going through a sudden, dramatic change in personality or appearance; preparing for death by making out a will or giving away possessions.[27]

What Can a Person Do?

Take it seriously. If someone mentions suicide or acts suicidal, go ahead and talk about it. Stay calm and be willing to listen. Show concern, but do not lecture or point out all the reasons a person has to live. Instead, ask questions about how the person feels and what plans he or she may have made. Do not worry that talking about it will encourage the person to go through with the plan; on the contrary, it will let him or her know that someone cares. It may save a life.

Get help immediately. Urge the person to call a suicide crisis line or suggest that he or she talk to a parent, teacher, counselor, minister, doctor, or other trusted adult. If the person does not get help right away, do so for him or her. This is not disloyalty. In fact, it could be the favor of a lifetime. Tell the person that life may seem tough at times, but the bad times never last forever.[28]

What Is the Bottom Line?

Young people who are suicidal are especially likely to have other problems—such as substance abuse, school problems, and physical or sexual abuse—that go along with their depression. Anyone who thinks about, threatens, or attempts suicide needs help right away. Treatment can be aimed not only at the depressed and suicidal feelings, but also at any other problems that may be involved.[29]

3

Home, School, and Work

Depression affects every part of a person's life. It can cause problems in the person's relationship with friends and family members. It can also cause a drop in how well the person functions at home, school, or work.[1] Teenagers may react to mental pain by getting into trouble. Depression can contribute to problems with grades, alcohol, drugs, sex, or out-of-control behavior.[2]

Depression at Home

Some teenagers who are depressed withdraw into their bedroom, cutting off contact with family members. Others get into constant arguments, responding to even small problems with angry outbursts. They may have more trouble controlling their temper at home than at school or at work.[3] Depressed teenagers may want to run away from home, and they may start to break rules and dress carelessly. Parents of such teenagers may complain that they are always grouchy or uncooperative.[4]

Depression at School

Grades often drop sharply as a result of depression because this disorder can hurt a student's ability to think clearly, pay attention, and remember things. When the student gets a bad grade, he or she may fall apart, seeing the grade as proof that he or she cannot do anything right. Some depressed teenagers refuse to go to school, often saying they feel sick. Others regularly sleep through classes, especially if they are abusing alcohol or drugs.[5] Still others get into frequent trouble at school.[6]

Depression at Work

Work performance can also suffer because of depression. Depressed people may miss a lot of work or have a poor attitude on the job. They may complain about being tired all the time or having vague aches and pains. They may also be particularly prone to safety problems and accidents at work.[7] It is estimated that Americans miss up to 200 million days of work each year because of depression. The value of lost work, plus the cost of treating depression, totals $30 billion to $44 billion a year.[8]

Depression at Play

Depressed teenagers often go to one extreme or another in their relationships. Many teenagers who are depressed retreat into their own world, cutting themselves off from friends. Others, however, spend every waking minute with friends, using constant social activity like a drug in an effort to dull their pain. Depression can take a heavy toll on friendship. It is no fun to be around someone who is gloomy or angry all the time. Also, some depressed teenagers are supersensitive to criticism. They may overreact to tiny slights, seeing them as signs of rejection.[9]

How Are Relationships Hurt?

Depressed people often push other people away. They may put themselves down or get angry easily. They may speak

Angela's Story

Angela is a seventeen-year-old high-school senior with a busy life. She is the editor of the school newspaper, and she is active in a special program to help students resolve conflicts. In the spring, she plays softball. Angela also works twenty hours a week as a waitress. In her spare time she enjoys writing in her journal, "chatting" with people online, and hanging out with her friends.

For the past two years, however, Angela has had occasional bouts of depression. When depressed, says Angela, "I find it a huge struggle to keep up with everything. Some days, I don't even feel like getting out of bed. I have to force myself to get up in the morning, or else I would sleep all the time."

Angela's relationships with others have suffered as a result. "It's like I don't know how to trust anyone," she says. Her grades have also slipped. "I used to be an honors student, but when I'm depressed, I have trouble just passing a test." Thanks to treatment with medicine and therapy over the past year, Angela is now doing better. Her advice to other teenagers: "You have to live day by day. Believe in yourself, and most importantly, trust that you have a bright and positive future ahead of you."[10]

in a slow, flat voice that is tough on the ears. Some talk about themselves too much. Others fail to respond or make eye contact. Still others scowl or frown all the time.[11]

To make matters worse, some teenagers who are depressed come from troubled families. Such teenagers and their parents may see their relationship as cold, angry, and tense.[12] Teenagers may fear that their parents do not care about them or will not understand their feelings. Unfortunately, this is sometimes true. Most parents are eager to help, though. If depressed teenagers need to talk, they should give their parents a chance to listen. If this does not work out, they can try a teacher, counselor, religious leader, doctor, or other trusted adult.

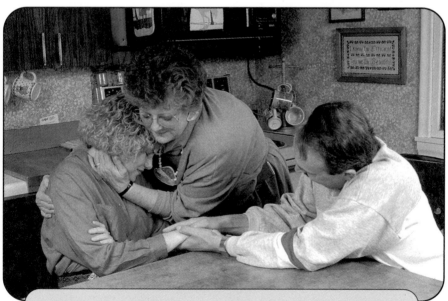

Talking to family members can help a person who is suffering from depression feel better.

Close friends can help make up for a less-than-perfect family life. However, depressed teenagers tend to pick friends who themselves have personal problems. These friends may be busy with their own crises, or they may have been put off by the teenager's behavior while depressed. Yet it helps to talk. If a depressed teenager needs support, he or she should reach out to a friend rather than shutting out all of the people who care.[13]

What About Substance Abuse?

Many depressed teenagers abuse alcohol or other drugs. Sometimes the depression occurs first. The person may be using alcohol or drugs as a way to escape the sadness. Other times, the alcohol or drug abuse occurs first. Depression may be caused by the drug itself, or it may be one of the withdrawal symptoms that occurs when the person stops using the drug. Depression may also be triggered by stresses that go along with alcohol or drug abuse, such as failure in school.

In any case, the sooner a person gets treatment for both these problems, the better. Either problem can make the other worse and lead to bigger problems, such as addiction.[14] Common warning signs of teen alcohol or drug abuse include a drop in grades, a change in friends, problems at home, and out-of-control behavior. Of course, all these symptoms can be caused by depression alone. When alcohol or drugs are involved, however, they often go along with physical signs, such as red eyes, a cough that does not go away, and a change in eating or sleeping habits. The risks of not getting help are too great to ignore. For people ages fifteen to twenty-four, half of all deaths are suicides, murders, or accidents that involve alcohol or drug abuse.[15]

Depression and Other Disorders

Depressed people can have other problems at the same time. In teenagers, depression often goes along with the following disorders:

- **substance abuse**—Regular use of alcohol or other drugs to the point that it causes serious problems. Some depressed teenagers turn to alcohol or drugs in an unsuccessful effort to ease their mental pain.

- **conduct disorder**—A long-standing pattern of harming or threatening others or breaking serious rules. Some teenagers try to distract themselves from depressed feelings by acting wild and taking risks.

- **anxiety disorder**—A feeling of uneasiness or fear and sometimes physical tension, even when no real threat exists. In children with both anxiety and depression, the anxiety disorder typically starts first, usually before age twelve. Such children often go on to develop a severe case of depression.[16]

- **eating disorders**—Severe problems in eating behavior, such as self-starvation or bingeing and purging. Either problem can start first and lead to the other. The symptoms of self-starvation and depression can be similar, including loss of appetite, poor concentration, and lack of energy.

- **attention deficit/hyperactivity disorder**—A lasting pattern of poor attention and/or overactive behavior. Young people with this disorder who are also becoming depressed often develop symptoms such as mood swings, withdrawal from other people, lack of energy, and trouble sleeping.

- **learning disabilities**—School achievement that is well below what would be expected based on intelligence. School problems can also be caused by the poor concentration and loss of interest that are signs of depression.[17]

What About Conduct Disorder?

Some depressed teenagers also have conduct disorder. This means they have a long-standing pattern of harming or threatening others or breaking serious rules. Teenagers with conduct disorder may be aggressive toward other people or animals. As a result, they may bully others, get into fights, use weapons, or commit violent crimes, such as muggings, armed robberies, or rapes. They may also destroy property, set fires, break into houses, lie, steal, break curfew, run away from home, or skip school. In short, they are constantly in big trouble.[18]

Teenagers with conduct disorder may take other risks as well, such as smoking, drinking, using drugs, or having casual sex. Their self-esteem is usually low, although they may mask this by acting and talking tough. Their lifestyle can lead to troubled relationships. It can also put these teenagers at high risk for arrest, injury, rape, alcohol or drug abuse, pregnancy, sexually transmitted diseases, and even murder. Treatment can help prevent such tragic outcomes.[19]

What Is the Bottom Line?

Young people who are depressed are highly likely to have other problems at the same time. The most common of these are substance abuse, conduct disorder, and anxiety.[20] Among young people whose depression is bad enough that they are admitted to a hospital, about four out of five have other problems. For such teenagers, treatment needs to be aimed at both the depression and the other problems.[21]

4

A Friend in Need

Depression saps energy and self-esteem. It can steal a person's ability or desire to get help. If a friend seems to be depressed, urge him or her to seek treatment. If he or she does not act soon, go ahead and talk to a trusted adult. This is particularly urgent if the friend mentions death or suicide. It is not a betrayal. In fact, it is a sign of true friendship to share such concerns with an adult who can help.[1]

Where Can Help Be Found?

Talk to a parent or another respected adult. If this is not an option, the telephone book should have numbers for a local crisis line or mental health center. Among the adults who may help are parents, other relatives, teachers, school counselors, school nurses, religious leaders, doctors, and therapists. Help may also be available from the following sources: a crisis hot line, a mental health center, a social service agency, or a support group.[2]

Lauren's Story

Lauren and her boyfriend, Scott, began dating as sophomores in high school. The two shared a common interest in music that drew them together. Soon, they felt closer to each other than to anyone else. By their junior year, however, something had gone wrong. "The sweet, fun boy I fell in love with was gone," says Lauren. In his place was a boy lost in deep despair. Sometimes Scott would lash out at Lauren. He also started drinking heavily, and he stopped playing the guitar.

By the summer before senior year, Scott talked constantly about death. "I asked him over and over to get help," says Lauren. "He did see a therapist once, but then he quit." Things came to a head one night when Scott showed up unexpectedly at Lauren's house. "He told me there was something for me in the glove box of his car," says Lauren. "I knew something was terribly wrong from the way he sounded." When Lauren looked in the glove box, she found a suicide note.

Lauren told her mother what was happening, and her mother called 911. Scott was taken to a hospital, where he was treated for severe depression and alcohol abuse. Lauren was afraid that Scott would never forgive her, but instead he thanked her for saving his life. Says Lauren, "It was an incredible lesson."[3]

What Else Can Be Done?

Let a depressed friend know that someone cares. Start a frank conversation about depression. Be a good listener, and urge the person to talk about how he or she feels. Accept his or her feelings without judging them. Do not lecture or criticize. Instead, encourage the person and offer reassurance. A depressed person needs to be reminded that things will eventually get better.

Learn more about depression. Then share this information with the person who is depressed. Tell him or her that effective treatments are available. Once the person gets professional help, stay supportive. Plan fun things to do together. Shop at the mall, go to a movie, grab a burger—anything to get the person out of the house.[4]

It is great to be a loyal buddy, but do not try to take responsibility for making another person well. Also, never

Talking to Friends

Here are some tips for being a good listener:

- Urge the person to talk.
- Listen without judging.
- Share a warm hug.
- Keep a positive attitude.
- Be open and honest.
- Do not act shocked.
- Stay cool and calm.
- Get help if needed.

Learning how to listen can be key to helping someone cope with the difficulties of depression.

agree to keep a friend's depressed state of mind a secret. If he or she might be suicidal, tell an adult right away.[5]

What Is the Bottom Line?

A depressed friend may need help to get help. Depression can make a person feel tired, worthless, and hopeless. Yet with proper treatment at least 80 percent of depressed people feel better, usually in a matter of weeks. The other 20 percent may eventually get better as well, once the right treatment is found. Share this good news with a person who is depressed. Give the great gift of hope for the future.[6]

5

Helpful, Hopeful Hints

People who are clinically depressed need professional treatment. Depression is an illness, and it cannot just be wished away. That does not mean that depressed people cannot help themselves. Here are some tips that may help depressed people speed up their recovery or ward off future attacks of depression.[1]

Exercise Regularly

Research has shown that exercise can lift the mood of many people with mild to moderate depression. No one is sure exactly how exercise has this effect. One theory is that exercise may lead to crucial changes in brain chemicals. Another theory is that simply moving the large muscles in regular, rhythmic ways may fight depression. To work against depression, exercise should be done for thirty minutes or longer at least three times a week. Five or more times a week is even better.

Walking and running are the most common forms of exercise used to treat depression. However, the same results can probably be gotten from other aerobic activities—continuous activities that use the large muscles of the arms and legs and make the heart beat faster. Other examples of aerobic activities include swimming laps, bicycling, and aerobic dancing.[2]

Eat Wisely

Good food helps the mind and body stay healthy and strong. Unfortunately, when people are depressed they may not feel like eating, or they may crave junk food.[3] Skipping meals just makes any problem with energy and concentration worse. Sugary foods may give an energy boost at first, but a few hours later they leave a person feeling more tired and cranky than ever.

A healthy diet also helps a person stay well and feel better in general. A good diet includes a variety of foods, including plenty of fruits, vegetables, and grains. It is low in fat and moderate in sugar and salt. Many teenagers need to eat more calcium-rich foods, such as low-fat or fat-free milk, cheese, and yogurt. Teenage girls should also make sure to eat enough iron-rich foods, such as lean meats and whole-grain or enriched white bread.[4]

Reduce Stress

Stress is not always a bad thing. Without a little stress, life would be dull and boring. Too much stress, however, can harm a person's mental and physical well-being. The critical thing is not so much what happens to a person but how the person reacts inside. For example, petting a golden

Research on St. John's wort

Some people claim that the herb hypericum, commonly known as St. John's wort, can relieve mild to moderate depression. It is widely used in Europe for this purpose. However, not enough scientific studies have yet been done to know if the herb really works and is safe. In the late 1990s, the National Institute of Mental Health began a large-scale three-year study to help answer these questions. Until the results are in, the Institute does not recommend the use of St. John's wort.[5]

retriever might be pleasant for most people, but for someone who is deathly afraid of dogs it would be very stressful. One way to reduce stress is simply to relax. When things get stressful, take a few moments to breathe deeply and imagine a restful scene, or create a quiet mood by reading a good book or playing beautiful music.[6]

A person who wants to relax can try this quick exercise: Lie down in a comfortable position. Think about breathing deeply. With the eyes closed, place one hand on the belly, just below the navel. With each breath in, feel the hand rise; with each breath out, feel the hand fall. Focus on the rising and falling hand for a few minutes. A good time to do this exercise is just before falling asleep at night. It can also be done during the day while sitting or standing.[7]

Stay Active

If a person is depressed, he or she may want to withdraw from other people and activities. Withdrawal just makes the sadness and loneliness worse, however. The person should try to spend time doing something fun with friends. To meet new friends, he or she can join a club or volunteer for an interesting cause.

When people's minds are not busy, they may dwell on depressing thoughts. Then they need activities to distract themselves. If they are depressed, they may not be able to

Self-Help for Depression

Once a person has gotten professional help for depression, what else can he or she do? Here are more tips for feeling better:

- Stay positive. Take depressed or hopeless thoughts with a grain of salt. The person should tell himself or herself, "That's just the depression talking."

- Keep alert. If a person has repeated attacks of depression, he or she should learn the warning signs and seek help before an attack becomes severe.

- Be patient. If a person is getting treatment, he or she should give it enough time to work and not expect to snap out of the depression overnight.[8]

- Make friends. The person might consider joining a support group.

- Get feedback. The person should ask friends and family whether they notice an improvement. Often, the person recovering from depression may not know how much better he or she seems.

- Be creative. The person can express himself or herself through writing, art, music, or drama. He or she should let out the feelings that are bottled up inside.

get as much done as usual. In this case, such people should not be too hard on themselves for failing to do everything. Instead, they should reward themselves for doing what they can.[9]

One good way to stay active is to set up a daily routine. This helps depressed people keep going when their energy is low. Setting and reaching goals can also make people feel

Michelle's Story

At age twelve, Michelle was faced with the birth of her sister, the death of her grandfather, and a move to a new town. It all felt like too much to handle, and she became depressed. "I felt worthless to the point where I hated it when people were nice to me because I didn't feel worthy," she says. It took months of treatment, plus support from her parents, to help Michelle recover.

That was three years ago. Today, at age fifteen, Michelle has learned to better deal with stress. One thing she does is write about her feelings. "I think that writing in a journal really helps with my depression," she says. "I may start off by simply writing, 'I want to die!' But then I begin to get into the deeper issue of why I'm feeling that way. It's very useful." She also writes stories and poems about depression. "It helps put feelings back in perspective when I write them down."

Another thing Michelle does is share her feelings online. "There are online message boards and chat rooms especially for depressed teens," she says. "I can't always talk to my school friends about depression, because they might not understand. But the people online are going through the same thing."[10]

Help on the Internet

Several Web sites dealing with depression are listed in the **For Further Information** section of this book. The following are some other sites that offer useful information and online support. Remember, though: Never give out personal information online. This includes full name, telephone number, and mailing address.

- Depression.com <http://depression.com>
- Internet Mental Health <http://www.mentalhealth.com>
- Mental Health Net <http://www.cmhc.com>
- Pendulum Resources <http://www.pendulum.org>

better about themselves. However, such people should make sure that the schedule allows time for rest and relaxation as well as for school and other activities.

What Is the Bottom Line?

People always feels better if they can help themselves. True depression is an illness, however. No one should try to treat it on his or her own.[11] People should seek professional help if they have several signs of depression that last for more than two weeks. They should also seek help if their thoughts and behavior change so much that they cannot keep up with normal activities.[12]

6

Help Is Out There

With proper treatment, at least four out of every five people with depression—even those with the most severe forms—feel better soon. Their symptoms usually improve in just a matter of weeks.[1] Unfortunately, two thirds of teenagers and children with mental health problems do not get the help they need. This is tragic because it causes much unnecessary suffering.[2]

Treatment helps keep depression from getting worse. It helps prevent depression from coming back, and it reduces mental pain and the risk of suicide. Likewise, treatment lets a person return to a normal life sooner.[3]

How Is Depression Diagnosed?

Before depression can be treated, it must be recognized. To check for depression and rule out other problems, a doctor must perform a complete medical exam. The doctor will

Kristin's Story

At age sixteen, Kristin was hospitalized for depression after a suicide attempt. After she was released, Kristin made regular visits to the hospital for therapy and medical checkups. This continued for just over a year. "I learned a lot," Kristin says. "One thing I learned was how an emotion such as sadness actually helps a person. I never cried much before. Now I cry occasionally, and I think it lets me release feelings so that I don't have to act them out in a negative way."

Along with depression, Kristin had a problem with drug abuse. She is now in a drug counseling program. She also takes part in a therapy group at a mental health center, and she is still on medication for depression. "I think treatment has helped me in many ways," she says. "I would tell other teens: 'It's a tough battle. The struggle is different for everyone, so you have to find what works best for you. But it's worth the effort. Without treatment, I might not be here today.'"[4]

also ask about present and past symptoms. In addition, the doctor may ask about any illnesses of other family members since many conditions, including major depression and bipolar disorder, tend to run in families.

If the doctor suspects that the problem is depression, he or she may send the person to another doctor or therapist who has been specially trained in treating mental health conditions. The doctor or therapist will try to find out if the person's mood, memory, or relationships have been affected.[5] One way to do this is by talking to the person and observing his or her behavior. Another way is with a paper-and-pencil test that asks the person to report his or her thoughts, feelings, and actions. Other family members may talk to the doctor or therapist as well.[6]

No simple lab test can check for depression; however, scientists are studying possible tests for depression, using blood, urine, spinal fluid, skin, brain waves, or brain images. The research is promising, but such tests are still experimental. They are not regularly used for this purpose.[7]

How Is Depression Treated?

Depression is usually treated with medication, psychotherapy, or both. Psychotherapy—also known as therapy or counseling—involves talking about feelings with a trained professional who can help the person change thoughts, actions, or relationships that play a part in the illness.[8]

Depression is usually treated in two steps. At first, the aim of treatment is to get rid of the symptoms of depression until the person feels well. After that, treatment is continued for a while to keep the depression from coming back. People who have had several bouts of depression may need to continue treatment longer. With proper treatment, the odds of staying well are excellent.

Treatment for depression works gradually over several weeks. With medication, most people feel better within three to four weeks. With psychotherapy, results can take a bit longer. It is important to give treatment enough time to work. If a treatment still is not working after a reasonable amount of time, it can be changed or another treatment can be tried. Almost everyone can be helped.[9]

What Newer Medications Are Used?

Several types of medication can be used to treat depression. These are known as antidepressants. Such medications are not addictive or habit-forming. Each works a little

Talking to a professional counselor can help change thoughts and feelings that play a part in depression.

differently.[10] In large groups of people, studies have found that the various kinds of depression medications, including both newer and older drugs, work about equally well. A given individual may find that one medication works better or worse for him or her, however. The doctor will try to find the medication that works best for a particular person and has the fewest unwanted side effects.[11]

Selective serotonin reuptake inhibitors (SSRIs) are a new class of antidepressants. The first SSRI, a drug called fluoxeline (Prozac), was first approved by the Food and Drug Administration in 1987.[12] SSRIs generally have fewer side effects than older kinds of antidepressants. At first, though, they can lead to anxiety, nervousness, sleep problems, stomach cramps, nausea, or skin rashes. In rare cases, they can cause sleepiness or even seizures.[13]

SSRIs work due to their action on a neurotransmitter, or natural brain chemical, known as serotonin. A second kind of new antidepressant affects both serotonin and another neurotransmitter, norepinephrine.

A third kind of new antidepressant is unrelated to other depression drugs.[14] These medications include bupropion (Wellbutrin) and trazodone (Desyrel). Like the other new medications, they are useful for people who are not helped by other antidepressants or who are bothered by their side effects.[15]

What Older Medications Are Used?

Heterocyclic antidepressants—once called tricyclic antidepressants—work well for up to four fifths of all people who are depressed. At first, they may cause side effects, such as blurred vision, constipation, dizziness, dry mouth, trouble urinating, and confusion. A small number of people have other side effects, such as sweating, racing heartbeat, low blood pressure, allergic skin reactions, and sensitivity to the sun. Any side effects usually go away after a few weeks. At this point, the person typically begins to feel better. Problems with sleep and energy clear up, and feelings of sadness and worthlessness lessen.

Monoamine oxidase inhibitors (MAOIs) work about as well as heterocyclic antidepressants. However, they are used less often because people who take them must eat a special diet. They have to avoid certain foods, such as cheese, beans, coffee, and chocolate. These foods contain a protein building block that can interact with the medication and cause a serious increase in blood pressure. MAOIs also interact with several other medications, yet they are sometimes useful for people who cannot take or are not helped by other antidepressants.[16]

What About Lithium?

Lithium is the drug most often used for treating the mania, or overly high mood, in bipolar disorder, the illness in which a person's mood swings from depression to mania and back again. Pure lithium is a naturally occurring mineral. It shows up in the water of certain springs. In earlier times, people "took the waters," drinking and bathing in lithium-rich water for its soothing effect.[17]

Lithium evens out mood swings. It usually lessens severe symptoms of mania in a week or two; however, it may be anywhere from days to months before the symptoms go away completely. If too little lithium is taken, the medication may not work well. If too much is taken, side effects may occur. Therefore, people taking lithium need regular blood tests to check the amount of drug in their body. Possible side effects include sleepiness, weakness, nausea, vomiting, tiredness, thirstiness, increased urination, and shakiness of the hands. These usually go away quickly, although the shaky hands may last longer. Weight gain can also occur.[18]

What About Psychotherapy?

Several kinds of psychotherapy are also used to treat depression, either alone or combined with medication. In psychotherapy, a person works with a trained professional who listens, talks, and helps the person solve problems. Psychotherapy for depression is usually fairly brief, often lasting for eight to twenty visits. Although it may start to work right away, it often takes eight to ten weeks for the full effects of therapy to be felt.

As with medication, different people react differently to various treatments. While many adults are helped by psychotherapy, others are not. Yet more than half of adults with mild to moderate depression get better with psychotherapy.

Adults with severe depression or bipolar disorder generally need medication; however, they may benefit from getting psychotherapy, too. A combination of medication and psychotherapy may be especially helpful for adults with long-lasting depression and those who have symptoms between full-fledged attacks. It is also useful for adults who do not get well with either medication or psychotherapy alone.[19]

For children and teenagers, psychotherapy is always recommended. A combination of medication and psychotherapy may be helpful for some young people, too, especially those with severe depression or bipolar disorder.[20]

What Psychotherapies Are Used?

Three kinds of psychotherapy have been well studied for the treatment of depression. Behavioral therapy focuses on current behaviors. Cognitive therapy focuses on thoughts and thinking patterns. Interpersonal therapy focuses on personal relationships. Other types of psychotherapy may also be helpful, but their value for depression has not been studied fully.[21]

Behavioral therapy is aimed at changing problem behaviors and thinking patterns. The person learns specific skills to get rewards and satisfaction. This can include learning to relax and manage stress. Behavioral therapy is often combined with cognitive therapy, in which the person learns to identify and change negative thinking patterns that can affect feelings and behavior.[22] Cognitive therapy was developed as a short-term treatment especially for depression, although it is now used for a wide range of problems.

Interpersonal therapy is another short-term treatment meant for depression. It focuses on the person's relationships with family members and friends. The person works on solving relationship problems that may play a role in depression, such as family conflicts, lack of social skills, life changes such as the move to high school, and grief over the death of a loved one.[23]

What About Electroconvulsive Therapy?

Electroconvulsive therapy—commonly known as ECT or shock therapy—involves sending carefully controlled pulses of electric current to the brain. This leads to brief seizures. Although it is not known why ECT works, it can help people with severe depression feel better quickly. For this reason, it may be used for people who have a high risk of suicide. ECT is also used for people with severe depression who are not helped by or cannot take medication.

ECT was first developed in the 1930s. At that time, it was still a risky treatment. Side effects included heart problems, serious memory loss, and even broken bones from the seizures. Today, doctors know how to prevent the worst side effects. Modern ECT is safe and painless.

A person who receives ECT is given drugs to put the person to sleep and relax the muscles. Then electrodes are placed on the head. Quick pulses of electric current are sent through the electrodes, causing brief seizures. The person does not feel this, though, because of the drugs. The whole process takes twenty to forty minutes. ECT for depression is usually given two or three times a week for a total of six to twelve treatments.[24]

What Other Treatments Are Used?

Light therapy—also called phototherapy—is sometimes used to treat people with mild to moderate seasonal affective disorder (SAD). It involves the use of special artificial lights that give people the effect of having a few extra hours of sunlight a day.[25] A person receiving light therapy sits a short distance from the special lights, which are much brighter than normal indoor lighting. This is done for several minutes to a few hours each day, often early in the morning or in the evening. Many people undergoing light therapy seem better in just a few days. However, more research is still needed on this treatment, and it should only be tried with professional guidance. Too much exposure to the strong lights may cause burns or eye damage.[26]

Hospitalization involves staying overnight in a hospital in which round-the-clock care is provided. Such a treatment is useful when depressed people are dangerous to themselves or to others. It is also helpful when symptoms are severe. Hospitalization may be particularly important for people who have attempted suicide or made suicide plans since they can be watched closely in this setting and kept from harming themselves. In addition to keeping these people safe, hospitalization makes it easy for the doctor to do a full set of medical and psychological tests. It also gives people and their families a chance to calm down if things have gotten seriously out of hand at home.[27]

What If Treatment Fails?

About one out of every five people treated for depression does not feel better within a short time.[28] When treatment fails, it is usually for one of these reasons: Psychotherapy did not continue for long enough, the type of psychotherapy or the therapist did not really suit the person's needs, medication was not taken for long enough, the dosage was not strong enough, the person did not fully cooperate in psychotherapy or take medication as prescribed, or the person had other mental or physical problems that needed a different treatment.

Even in such difficult cases, however, a change in treatment will often bring better results. One good thing about depression is that there are many different kinds of treatment that can be tried. Almost everyone can be helped eventually.[29]

What Is the Last Word?

Depression is one of the most common and painful of all mental health problems. Fortunately, it is also one of the most treatable. No one needs to fight depression alone.[30]

For Further Information

* Indicates a support group. Check the local telephone book, or call the national office of these groups to find a nearby meeting.

§ Indicates a group for mental health professionals. These groups can provide more details on the various helping professions.

American Academy of Child and Adolescent Psychiatry §
3615 Wisconsin Ave., N.W.
Washington, DC 20016-3007
(202) 966-7300
<http://www.aacap.org>

American Foundation for Suicide Prevention
120 Wall St., 22nd Floor
New York, NY 10005
(888) 333-AFSP
<http://www.afsp.org>

Depression and Related Affective Disorders Association *
Meyer 3-181, 600 N. Wolfe St.
Baltimore, MD 21287-7381
(410) 955-4647
<http://www.med.jhu.edu/drada>

National Institute of Mental Health
5600 Fishers Lane
Rockville, MD 20857
(800) 421-4211
<http://www.nimh.nih.gov/depression/index.htm>

National Alliance for Research on Schizophrenia and Depression
60 Cutter Mill Road, Suite 404
Great Neck, NY 11021
(516) 829-0091
(800) 829-8289
<http://www.mhsource.com/narsad.html>

National Alliance for the Mentally Ill *
200 N. Glebe Road, Suite 1015
Arlington, VA 22203-3754
(800) 950-NAMI
<http://www.nami.org>

National Depressive and Manic-Depressive Association *
730 N. Franklin St., Suite 501
Chicago, IL 60610-3526
(800) 82-NDMDA
<http://www.ndmda.org>

National Foundation for Depressive Illness, Inc.
P.O. Box 2257
New York, NY 10116
(800) 239-1265
<http://www.depression.org>

National Mental Health Association
1021 Prince St.
Alexandria, VA 22314-2971
(800) 969-NMHA
<http://www.nmha.org>

Chapter Notes

Chapter 1. Blues, Blahs, or Depression?

1. American Psychiatric Association, "Let's Talk Facts About Depression" (Washington, D.C.: American Psychiatric Association, 1994).

2. Depression/Awareness, Recognition, and Treatment, "Let's Talk About Depression" (Rockville, Md.: National Institute of Mental Health, 1997), NIH Publication No. 97-4162.

3. National Center for Injury Prevention and Control, "Ten Leading Causes of Death, United States, 1993–95," 1998, <http://www.cdc.gov/ncipc/osp/leadcaus/ustable.htm> (October 16, 1998).

4. E-mails from "Justin" to the author, October 16 and 18, 1998. ("Justin" is a real person, but his name and a few identifying details have been changed to protect his privacy.)

5. American Psychiatric Association, *Diagnostic and Statistical Manual of Mental Disorders*, 4th ed. (Washington, D.C.: American Psychiatric Association, 1994), p. 327.

6. American Psychiatric Association, "Let's Talk Facts About Depression."

7. American Psychiatric Association, *Diagnostic and Statistical Manual of Mental Disorders*, pp. 325, 341.

8. Center for Mental Health Services, "Major Depression in Children and Adolescents" (Rockville, Md.: Center for Mental Health Services, 1996).

9. American Psychiatric Association, *Diagnostic and Statistical Manual of Mental Disorders*, p. 389.

10. American Psychiatric Association, "Let's Talk Facts About Depression."

11. Norman E. Rosenthal, M.D., *Winter Blues: Seasonal Affective Disorder—What It Is and How to Overcome It* (New York: Guilford, 1998), pp. 3, 62.

12. American Psychiatric Association, *Diagnostic and Statistical Manual of Mental Disorders*, p. 349.

13. Depression/Awareness, Recognition, and Treatment, "Bipolar Disorder" (Rockville, Md.: National Institute of Mental Health, 1995), NIH Publication No. 95-3679.

14. American Psychiatric Association, *Diagnostic and Statistical Manual of Mental Disorders*, p. 332.

15. American Academy of Child and Adolescent Psychiatry, "Manic-Depressive Illness in Teens" (Washington, D.C.: American Academy of Child and Adolescent Psychiatry, 1995).

16. American Psychiatric Association, *Diagnostic and Statistical Manual of Mental Disorders*, p. 332.

17. Ibid., pp. 317, 768.

18. Allen Frances, M.D., Michael B. First, M.D., and Harold Alan Pincus, M.D., *Diagnostic and Statistical Manual of Mental Disorders Handbook of Differential Diagnosis* (Washington, D.C.: American Psychiatric Press, 1995), pp. 155–156.

19. National Alliance for Research on Schizophrenia and Depression, "Conquering Depression" (Great Neck, N.Y.: National Alliance for Research on Schizophrenia and Depression, 1996).

20. Ellen Hughes, "Depression," 1998, <http://www.ama-assn.org/insight/spec_con/depressn/depressn.htm> (October 18, 1998).

21. Center for Mental Health Services.

22. Depression: Treat it. Defeat it., n.d., <http://www.nimh.nih.gov/dart1/genpop/gen_fact.htm> (May 24, 1999).

23. Depression/Awareness, Recognition, and Treatment, "Depression: What Every Woman Should Know" (Rockville, Md.: National Institute of Mental Health, 1995), NIH Publication No. 95-3871.

24. American Psychiatric Association, *Diagnostic and Statistical Manual of Mental Disorders*, pp. 387, 717.

25. Susan Nolen-Hoeksema, and Joan S. Girgus, "Worried Girls: Rumination and the Transition into Adolescence," presented at the 106th Annual Convention of the American Psychological Association, San Francisco, Calif., August 1998.

26. American Psychiatric Association, *Diagnostic and Statistical Manual of Mental Disorders*, p. 341.

27. Depression/Awareness, Recognition, and Treatment, "Let's Talk About Depression."

Chapter 2. Yellow Lights, Red Flags

1. American Psychiatric Association, *Diagnostic and Statistical Manual of Mental Disorders*, 4th ed. (Washington, D.C.: American Psychiatric Association, 1994), pp. 320–323, 327.

2. Barbara D. Ingersoll and Sam Goldstein, *Lonely, Sad, and Angry: A Parent's Guide to Depression in Children and Adolescents* (New York: Doubleday, 1995), pp. 5–6.

3. Gail A. Bernstein et al., "Somatic Symptoms in Anxious-Depressed School Refusers," *Journal of the American Academy of Child and Adolescent Psychiatry*, vol. 36, no. 5, May 1997, pp. 661–668.

4. Depression/Awareness, Recognition, and Treatment, "Let's Talk About Depression" (Rockville, Md.: National Institute of Mental Health, 1997), NIH Publication No. 97-4162.

5. Ingersoll and Goldstein, p. 6.

6. American Psychiatric Association, *Diagnostic and Statistical Manual of Mental Disorders*, pp. 321, 327.

7. Ingersoll and Goldstein, p. 6.

8. American Psychiatric Association, *Diagnostic and Statistical Manual of Mental Disorders*, pp. 321, 389.

9. Ingersoll and Goldstein, p. 7.

10. American Psychiatric Association, *Diagnostic and Statistical Manual of Mental Disorders*, p. 321.

11. Allen Frances, M.D., Michael B. First, M.D., and Harold Alan Pincus, M.D., *Diagnostic and Statistical Manual of Mental Disorders Guidebook* (Washington, D.C.: American Psychiatric Press, 1995), p. 197.

12. American Psychiatric Association, *Diagnostic and Statistical Manual of Mental Disorders*, p. 321.

13. Ingersoll and Goldstein, pp. 7–8.

14. Depression/Awareness, Recognition, and Treatment.

15. Ingersoll and Goldstein, p. 8.

16. American Psychiatric Association, *Diagnostic and Statistical Manual of Mental Disorders*, p. 322.

17. Ingersoll and Goldstein, p. 8.

18. Frances, First, and Pincus, p. 198.

19. Ingersoll and Goldstein, p. 9.

20. Frances, First, and Pincus, p. 198.

21. Depression/Awareness, Recognition, and Treatment.

22. American Academy of Child and Adolescent Psychiatry, "Mental Health Fact Sheet" (Washington, D.C.: American Academy of Child and Adolescent Psychiatry, 1998).

23. American Foundation for Suicide Prevention, "Child and Adolescent Suicide" (New York: American Foundation for Suicide Prevention, 1998).

24. American Psychiatric Association, "Teen Suicide" (Washington, D.C.: American Psychiatric Association, 1997).

25. American Foundation for Suicide Prevention.

26. American Psychiatric Association, "Teen Suicide."

27. American Association of Suicidology, "Suicide in Youth: What You Can Do about It" (Washington, D.C.: American Association of Suicidology, 1998).

28. Ibid.

29. American Academy of Child and Adolescent Psychiatry, "Practice Parameters for the Assessment and Treatment of Children and Adolescents with Depressive Disorders," *Journal of the American Academy of Child and Adolescent Psychiatry*, vol. 37, suppl. 10, October 1998, pp. 63S–83S.

Chapter 3. Home, School, and Work

1. American Psychiatric Association, *Diagnostic and Statistical Manual of Mental Disorders*, 4th ed. (Washington, D.C.: American Psychiatric Association, 1994), p. 327.

2. Depression/Awareness, Recognition, and Treatment, "Let's Talk About Depression" (Rockville, Md.: National Institute of Mental Health, 1997), NIH Publication No. 97-4162.

3. Barbara D. Ingersoll and Sam Goldstein, *Lonely, Sad, and Angry: A Parent's Guide to Depression in Children and Adolescents* (New York: Doubleday, 1995), pp. 5–6, 20.

4. Depression and Related Affective Disorders Association, "Adolescent Depression: A Counselor's Guide" (Baltimore: Depression and Related Affective Disorders Association, 1998).

5. Ingersoll and Goldstein, pp. 8, 19, 167, 169.

6. Depression/Awareness, Recognition, and Treatment, "Let's Talk About Depression."

7. Depression/Awareness, Recognition, and Treatment, "Depression: Effective Treatments Are Available" (Rockville, Md.: National Institute of Mental Health, 1996), NIH Publication No. 96-3590.

8. Ingersoll and Goldstein, pp. 8, 20, 163.

9. Depression/Awareness, Recognition, and Treatment, "D/ART General Information," n.d., <http://www.nimh.nih.gov/dart/gen_fact.htm> (October 16, 1998).

10. E-mails from "Angela" to the author, November 5, 1998. ("Angela" is a real person, but her name and a few identifying details have been changed to protect her privacy.)

11. R. Brian Giesler, Robert A. Josephs, and William B. Swann, Jr., "Self-Verification in Clinical Depression: The Desire for Negative Evaluation," *Journal of Abnormal Psychology*, vol. 105, no. 3, August 1996, pp. 358–368.

12. Ingersoll and Goldstein, pp. 64–65.

13. Ibid., p. 127.

14. Depression/Awareness, Recognition, and Treatment, "Let's Talk About Depression."

15. American Academy of Child and Adolescent Psychiatry, "Glossary of Symptoms and Mental Illnesses Affecting Teenagers" (Washington, D.C.: American Academy of Child and Adolescent Psychiatry, 1997).

16. Ingersoll and Goldstein, pp. 26–31.

17. American Psychiatric Association, pp. 46, 83–84, 90, 182, 325, 539, 764.

18. American Psychiatric Association, *Diagnostic and Statistical Manual of Mental Disorders*, p. 90.

19. Ingersoll and Goldstein, pp. 32–33.

20. American Academy of Child and Adolescent Psychiatry, "Practice Parameters for the Assessment and Treatment of Children and Adolescents with Depressive Disorders," *Journal of the American Academy of Child and Adolescent Psychiatry*, vol. 37, suppl. 10, October 1998, pp. 63S–83S.

21. Ingersoll and Goldstein, p. 25.

Chapter 4. A Friend in Need

1. Depression/Awareness, Recognition, and Treatment, "What to Do When a Friend Is Depressed: Guide for Students" (Rockville, Md.: National Institute of Mental Health, 1994), NIH Publication No. 94-3824.

2. Depression/Awareness, Recognition, and Treatment, "Let's Talk About Depression" (Rockville, Md.: National Institute of Mental Health, 1997), NIH Publication No. 97-4162.

3. Personal communication from "Lauren" to the author, November 19, 1998. ("Lauren" is a real person, but her name and a few identifying details have been changed to protect her privacy.)

4. Ellen Hughes, "Depression," 1998, <http://www.ama-assn.org/insight/spec_con/depressn/depressn.htm> (October 18, 1998).

5. National Depressive and Manic-Depressive Association, "Just a Mood . . . or Real Depression?" (Chicago: National Depressive and Manic-Depressive Association, 1996).

6. Depression/Awareness, Recognition, and Treatment, "Depression: Effective Treatments Are Available" (Rockville, Md.: National Institute of Mental Health, 1996), NIH Publication No. 96-3590.

Chapter 5. Helpful, Hopeful Hints

1. Ellen Hughes, "Depression," 1998, <http://www.ama-assn.org/insight/spec_con/depressn/depressn.htm> (October 18, 1998).

2. John H. Greist, M.D. and James W. Jefferson, M.D., *Depression and Its Treatment*, rev. ed. (Washington, D.C.: American Psychiatric Press, 1992), pp. 77–78.

3. American Psychiatric Association, *Diagnostic and Statistical Manual of Mental Disorders*, 4th ed. (Washington, D.C.: American Psychiatric Association, 1994), p. 321.

4. U.S. Department of Agriculture, "Dietary Guidelines for Americans," 4th ed. (Washington, D.C.: U.S. Department of Agriculture, 1995), Home and Garden Bulletin No. 232.

5. National Institute of Mental Health, "Questions and Answers About St. John's Wort," 1997, <http://www.nimh.nih.gov/publicat/stjohnqa.htm> (November 4, 1998).

6. Louis E. Kopolow, M.D., "Plain Talk about Handling Stress" (Bethesda, Md.: National Institute of Mental Health, 1991), DHHS Publication No. 91-502.

7. Herbert Benson, M.D. and Eileen M. Stuart, *The Wellness Book: The Comprehensive Guide to Maintaining Health and Treating Stress-Related Illness* (New York: Simon & Schuster, 1992), pp. 41–42.

8. Frederic I. Kass, M.D., John M. Oldham, M.D., and Herbert Pardes, M.D., eds., *The Columbia University College of Physicians and Surgeons Complete Home Guide to Mental Health* (New York: Henry Holt, 1992), p. 122.

9. Ibid., p. 122.

10. E-mails from "Michelle" to the author, October 20 and November 17, 1998. ("Michelle" is a real person, but her name and a few identifying details have been changed to protect her privacy.)

11. National Mental Health Association, "Depression: What You Need to Know" (Alexandria, Va.: National Mental Health Association, 1996).

12. Depression/Awareness, Recognition, and Treatment, "Helpful Facts About Depressive Illnesses" (Rockville, Md.: National Institute of Mental Health, 1997), NIH Publication No. 97-3875.

Chapter 6. Help Is Out There

1. Depression/Awareness, Recognition, and Treatment, "Depression: Effective Treatments Are Available" (Rockville, Md.: National Institute of Mental Health, 1996), NIH Publication No. 96-3590.

2. National Mental Health Association, "Childhood Depression Awareness Day: Factsheet" (Alexandria, Va.: National Mental Health Association, 1998).

3. Agency for Health Care Policy and Research, "Depression Is a Treatable Illness: A Patient's Guide" (Silver Spring, Md.: Agency for Health Care Policy and Research, 1993), AHCPR Publication No. 93-0553.

4. E-mails from "Kristin" to the author, October 10 and 23, 1998. ("Kristin" is a real person, but her name and a few identifying details have been changed to protect her privacy.)

5. Depression/Awareness, Recognition, and Treatment, "Helpful Facts About Depressive Illnesses" (Rockville, Md.: National Institute of Mental Health, 1997), NIH Publication No. 97-3875.

6. John H. Greist, M.D. and James W. Jefferson, M.D., *Depression and Its Treatment*, rev. ed. (Washington, D.C.: American Psychiatric Press, 1992), pp. 26, 35.

7. Frederic I. Kass, M.D., John M. Oldham, M.D., and Herbert Pardes, M.D., eds., *The Columbia University College of Physicians and Surgeons Complete Home Guide to Mental Health* (New York: Henry Holt, 1992), p. 113.

8. Depression/Awareness, Recognition, and Treatment, "Let's Talk About Depression" (Rockville, Md.: National Institute of Mental Health, 1997), NIH Publication No. 97-4162.

9. Agency for Health Care Policy and Research, "Depression Is a Treatable Illness."

10. Ibid.

11. Agency for Health Care Policy and Research, "Treatment of Depression: Newer Pharmacotherapies" (Silver Spring, Md.: Agency for Health Care Policy and Research, 1999), AHCPR Publication No. 99-E013.

12. Michael D. Lemonick, "Medicine: The Mood Molecule," *Time*, September 29, 1997, pp. 74+.

13. American Psychiatric Association, "Let's Talk Facts About Depression" (Washington, D.C.: American Psychiatric Association, 1994).

14. National Institute of Mental Health, "Medications" (Bethesda, Md.: National Institute of Mental Health, 1995), NIH Publication No. 95-3929.

15. Kass, Oldham, and Pardes, p. 72.

16. American Psychiatric Association, "Psychiatric Medications" (Washington, D.C.: American Psychiatric Association, 1997).

17. National Institute of Mental Health, "Lithium" (Bethesda, Md.: National Institute of Mental Health, 1993), NIH Publication No. 93-3476.

18. National Institute of Mental Health, "Medications."

19. Agency for Health Care Policy and Research, "Depression Is a Treatable Illness."

20. American Academy of Child and Adolescent Psychiatry, "Practice Parameters for the Assessment and Treatment of Children and Adolescents with Depressive Disorders," *Journal of the American Academy of Child and Adolescent Psychiatry*, vol. 37, suppl. 10, October 1998, pp. 63S–83S.

21. Agency for Health Care Policy and Research, "Depression in Primary Care: Detection, Diagnosis, and Treatment" (Silver Spring, Md.: Agency for Health Care Policy and Research, 1993), AHCPR Publication No. 93-0552.

22. Center for Mental Health Services, "A Consumer's Guide to Mental Health Services" (Rockville, Md.: Center for Mental Health Services, 1994), NIH Publication No. 94–3585.

23. Kass, Oldham, and Pardes, p. 118.

24. Ibid., pp. 78–79.

25. Agency for Health Care Policy and Research, "Depression Is a Treatable Illness."

26. Kass, Oldham, and Pardes, p. 79.

27. Barbara D. Ingersoll and Sam Goldstein, *Lonely, Sad, and Angry: A Parent's Guide to Depression in Children and Adolescents* (New York: Doubleday, 1995), pp. 133–138.

28. Depression/Awareness, Recognition, and Treatment, "Depression: Effective Treatments Are Available."

29. American Academy of Child and Adolescent Psychiatry.

30. American Psychiatric Association, "Let's Talk Facts About Depression" (Washington, D.C.: American Psychiatric Association, 1994).

Glossary

antidepressant—Drug used to treat depression.

behavioral therapy—Psychotherapy that focuses on current behaviors.

bipolar disorder—An illness in which a person's mood swings from depression to mania and back again, with normal periods in between. The mood extremes may be mild or severe, and the mood changes may occur slowly or quickly. Also known as manic depression.

clinical depression—Depression that is severe enough to need treatment.

cognitive therapy—Psychotherapy that focuses on thoughts and thinking patterns.

depression—An illness in which a person either feels low or loses interest in nearly all activities; this mood lasts for at least two weeks. The person also has several other symptoms, such as feelings of worthlessness, thoughts of death, or changes in eating, sleeping, thinking, movement, or energy level. Also known as major depression or clinical depression.

dysthymia—An illness in which a person has a low mood that is milder and involves fewer symptoms than major depression but lasts for at least a year or two.

electroconvulsive therapy—A treatment that involves sending carefully controlled pulses of electric current to the brain, which leads to brief seizures. It is a fast treatment for severe depression. Commonly known as ECT or shock therapy.

heterocyclic antidepressant—An older class of drug used to treat depression. Formerly known as tricyclic antidepressant.

hospitalization—Staying overnight in a hospital in which constant care is provided for depression.

interpersonal therapy—Psychotherapy that focuses on personal relationships.

light therapy—Involves the use of special artificial lights that give people the effect of having a few extra hours of sunlight a day. It is used to treat seasonal affective disorder. Also known as phototherapy.

major depression—Formal name for depression.

mania—An overly high or irritable mood that lasts for at least one week or leads to dangerous behavior. The person in a manic mood also has several other symptoms, such as inflated self-esteem, risk-taking behavior, or changes in sleeping, talking, thinking, or activity level.

manic depression—Common name for bipolar disorder.

monoamine oxidase inhibitor (MAOI)—An older class of drug used to treat depression.

mood—A long-lasting emotion that colors the way a person sees the world.

mood disorder—A mental illness in which the main feature is an abnormal mood. Depression, dysthymia, bipolar disorder, and seasonal affective disorder are examples of mood disorders.

neurotransmitters—Natural chemicals that let brain cells talk with one another. These chemicals may be out of balance in depression.

postpartum depression—Depression that occurs in women within four weeks after giving birth.

psychotherapy—Involves talking about feelings with a trained professional who can help the person change thoughts, actions, or relationships that play a part in mental illness. Also known as therapy or counseling.

seasonal affective disorder (SAD)—Depression in which the symptoms come in the fall or winter and leave in the spring. It seems to be linked to the decreased amount of sunlight that is available as the days grow shorter in winter.

selective serotonin reuptake inhibitor (SSRI)—A new class of drugs used to treat depression.

St. John's wort—Common name for the herb hypericum. This herb is being studied as a possible natural treatment for depression.

Further Reading

Carter, Sharon, and Lawrence Clayton. *Coping with Depression.* Center City, Minn.: Hazelden, 1995.

Cobain, Bev. *When Nothing Matters Anymore: A Survival Guide for Depressed Teens.* Minneapolis: Free Spirit, 1998.

Garland, E. Jane, M.D. *Depression Is the Pits, but I'm Getting Better: A Guide for Adolescents.* Washington, D.C.: Magination, 1997.

Irwin, Cait. *Depression: Challenge the Beast Within Yourself . . . and Win.* 2nd ed. Dallas: AVI Communications, 1998.

Silverstein, Alvin, and Virginia and Laura Silverstein Nunn. *Depression.* Springfield, N.J.: Enslow Publishers, 1997.

Internet Resources

See also the Web sites of groups in the **For Further Information** section of this book.

Agency for Healthcare Research and Quality
<http://www.ahcpr.gov>

American Academy of Child and Adolescent Psychiatry, "Summary of the Practice Parameters for the Assessment and Treatment of Children and Adolescents with Depressive Disorders"
<http://www.aacap.org/clinical/Depres~1.htm>

American Association of Suicidology, "Suicide in Youth: What You Can Do About It"
<http://www.suicidology.org/suicide_in_youth.htm>

American Psychiatric Association
<http://www.psych.org>

National Alliance for Research on Schizophrenia and Depression, "Conquering Depression"
<http://www.mhsource.com/advocacy/narsad/dep.html>

National Depressive and Manic-Depressive Association, "Just a Mood . . . or Something Else? . . .: A Brochure for Teens About Depressive Illnesses"
<http://www.ndmda.org/justmood.htm>

National Institute of Mental Health, "Medications"
<http://www.nimh.nih.gov/publicat/medicate.htm>

National Mental Health Association, "Childhood Depression Awareness Day"
<http://www.nmha.org/children/green>

Index

A
antidepressants, 41 (*see also* medications)
anxiety disorder, 27, 28
attention deficit/hyperactivity disorder, 27

B
behavioral therapy, 45
Bernstein, Gail, 15
bipolar disorder, 8–10, 44, 45

C
clinical depression, 7 (*see also* depression, major)
cognitive therapy, 45
conduct disorder, 27, 28

D
death, thoughts of, 7, 18
depressed mood, 5, 6–7, 7–8, 14–15
depression, major, 6–7, 10
Desyrel, 43
diagnosis, 39–41
diet, 34
dysthymia, 7–8, 10

E
eating, changes in, 7, 8, 15–16
eating disorders, 27
electroconvulsive therapy, 46
energy, changes in, 7, 8, 9, 17
exercise, 33–34

F
family, relationship with, 5, 8, 11, 15, 22–23, 24–25, 45–46
friends, relationship with, 5, 8, 15, 23–25, 26, 29–32, 35–36,45–46

G
gender differences, 12–13
grief, 11, 46

H
heterocyclic antidepressants, 43
hormones, 11, 12
hospitalization, 28, 47

I
interest, loss of, 6, 15
Internet resources, 38
interpersonal therapy, 45–46

L
learning disabilities, 27
light therapy, 46–47
lithium, 44

M
mania, 8–10, 44
manic depression, 8 (*see also* bipolar disorder)
medications, 41–44, 44–45, 47
monoamine oxidase inhibitors, 43
mood, 10

mood disorders, 10
movement, changes in, 7, 9, 11, 16

N
neurotransmitters, 11, 43
Nolen-Hoeksema, Susan, 12–13
norepinephrine, 43

P
phototherapy, 46 (*see also* light therapy)
physical abuse, 21
physical symptoms, 14–15
postpartum depression, 12
Prozac, 42
psychotherapy, 41, 44–46, 47

R
risk-taking behavior, 8–9, 9–10, 28

S
school, 5, 8, 11, 21, 23, 27
seasonal affective disorder, 7, 10, 16, 46–47
selective serotonin reuptake inhibitors, 42–43

serotonin, 43
sexual abuse, 21
sexual behavior, 5, 9, 28
shock therapy, 46 (*see also* electroconvulsive therapy)
sleeping, changes in, 7, 8, 9, 16
St. John's wort, 35
stress, 11, 12, 34–35
substance abuse, 5, 20, 21, 23, 26, 28
suicide, 5, 11, 18, 20–21, 26, 27, 47
support groups, 30, 36, 49, 50

T
thinking, changes in, 7, 8, 9, 17–18
treatment, 7, 21, 26, 28, 29, 31, 32, 33, 36, 39–48
tricyclic antidepressants, 43

W
warning signs, 18, 20, 26
Wellbutrin, 43
work, 8, 11, 23
worthlessness, feelings of, 7, 8, 11, 17